SPIRITUAL PASSPORT

Finding the Answer

by
Clara & Sebastian Naum

Illustrated by
Sebastian Naum & Aida Shabani

ISBN: 1480003492
ISBN 13: 9781480003491
Library of Congress Control Number: 2012918299
CreateSpace Independent Publishing Platform
North Charleston, South Carolina

A gift for:

....

From:

....

Para Verónica y
Mario
con mucho

Clau

dec-14

This book is dedicated to every child in the world, including the child inside each of us, who is eager to find answers to life's deepest truths.

Our intention is to inspire children and adults alike with a book that is inspirational and educational, yet simple enough that it touches peoples' hearts with a message of peace, love, and wonder. We intend to invite the reader to embark on a journey that will forever change the way they see the world.

With Love and Peace,

Clara & Sebastian
Irvine, California
2013

Acknowledgements

First and foremost, we are grateful to God for the miracle of our existence and the inner power that allowed us to complete this book, even in the middle of strong storms in our lives.

We are grateful to our parents, who supported us during our own adventures, and showed us love along the way.

We want also to express our gratitude to our son, Seba, and his continuing love and support during this project.

To Laura, Sebastian's sister, who fell in love with our book the very first time she read it and gave us much valuable feedback.

We also want to express our gratitude to Aida Shabani, who patiently accepted and interpreted the numerous changes we made along the way to make Tian and Lara the way they are now.

To all of you, much love and many thanks,

Clara & Sebastian

Contents

The Question

It was summer, the sun was shining, and Lara and Tian were enjoying the heat. School was over and they had all the time in the world to explore and play. Tian usually spent most summers at his grandparents' house. Their small, neat, white picket fence cottage was near the beach in a small town in northern California.

He loved spending time playing around the house, going for long walks with his grandparents, and spending Sundays at the local fair, but what he loved the most was the time spent with Lara.

Lara lived with her parents in a beautiful yellow house next to Tian's grandparents. They had a huge backyard filled with flowers, fruit trees, and a colorful Indian canopy tent that Lara's father had built for her when she was little.

Tian and Lara had known each other since they were very young and had always enjoyed each other's company. Neither of them had siblings, so they longed for this time together during the long summer days. They played games, talked about school and friends, and roamed around their huge backyards, but what they enjoyed the most was spending time in their small Indian tent.

The Indian tent was where they hid their treasures. The shells they had collected on the beach were used as decoration, the books that Lara loved were in the bottom right corner, and the walls were covered with the drawings that Lara and Tian had made along the years. The greatest thing about this tent, though, was that it was where they had their imaginary adventures.

Tian loved to play sports, and it wasn't easy for him to be quiet or stay put, but when he was with Lara during the summers, he would spend hours listening to her stories. Lara was a fun girl to be around, always smiling and curious about learning. She was always reading something that she wanted to share with Tian, who would in turn listen to her with eyes wide open. Summers were for enjoyment and discovery.

However, this was a different summer. Lara was about to start junior high. That meant going to a different school and meeting new friends. Tian still had one year to go, but his family was moving to a nearby city, which also meant a different school for him. They were eager to talk to each other and tell their stories.

They were both a lot bigger this year than last year, and as they grew, the tent seemed to shrink. This year, they wanted more space. They had been dreaming about having a tree house somewhere in the large wooded backyard, where they could spend time and have new imaginary adventures.

This time, the expedition was going to be different from all the previous ones. No monsters, princesses, or superheroes were going to be part of this adventure. This time, they were about to embark on their most memorable journey. They would go in search of a hidden treasure: *the answer to their questions.*

One morning, Lara and Tian were playing catch in Tian's huge backyard, hiding behind trees and bushes, giggling, talking, and playing.

"I really love it when you come here every summer, Tian. I like going on adventures with you. Each summer, we learn something exciting and new."

"I know, but this summer I don't feel like I'm learning much." Tian frowned.

"Are you OK? You look a little bummed out."

As Tian caught and threw the ball back to Lara, he thought about how he saw her as the big sister he didn't have. He thought about how much he had learned since he met her years and years ago. He was a little distracted and absorbed in his own thoughts—that was something that didn't happen very often when he was with Lara.

For a while now, he'd been wondering what life was really about. The previous school year, one of his good friends had become very sick. That had made Tian very sad, as well as more aware of things he'd never had to think about before.

He thought that Lara might be able to help with his doubts and concerns. "I'm just confused. I have a lot of questions and no answers..." Tian said, his big eyes staring at Lara.

"What kind of questions?" Lara asked with her head tilted.

"About life. What are we on earth for? What is life about?" he replied.

"What do you mean?" Lara asked.

"I always hear my parents and their friends talking about doing things to live a better life"

"You're right!" Lara exclaimed. "I've heard many people talk about how to live a better life. I saw Oprah on TV talking about it, as well as Chopra, Marianne Williamson, Wayne Dyer, Louise Hay, Don Miguel Ruiz, and many others."

"Whoa!" Tian said. "What team do they play for?"

Lara laughed. "No, Tian. They're not part of any sports team. They're all *very* important people who talk about *very* important things, like being better humans and about what people are here for."

"Oh, cool! Well, let's call Oprah and ask her what she does to live a better life."

Lara laughed again and patted Tian on the shoulder. "I wish it were that easy! Maybe one day we will." She smiled. "Why not?"

The Idea

....

Lara and Tian were sitting under one of the largest trees in the backyard. Nekty, an old orange-bellied turtle that Lara loved very much, was seated next to Tian. Nekty had shown up at the doorstep of a summer cottage in Florida where Lara and her parents spent a summer vacation years ago. As soon as Lara saw Nekty, she knew she was going to be her companion. She begged her parents to take the old turtle back to California with them. Lara's father joked about Nekty's long wrinkled neck saying that Lara should make a necktie for the turtle to make her look fancy. Lara made one for her, and thought that the turtle was cute with her necktie, and decided to call her "Nekty." Nekty had been Lara's pet from that moment on. She didn't require much attention, and spent the summers wandering outside, looking for bugs, slugs, and worms. During winter, Nekty always left, but Lara knew that she would show up again when it was warm, ready to be part of their summer adventures.

"So, if *so* many people want to know about how to live a better life, who has the answer?" Tian asked while petting Nekty's hard shell.

"I have an idea," Lara said enthusiastically. "Let's travel through time and space to find different answers that can help us live better lives!"

"Wait, what?" Tian asked.

"Yes! We can travel to the past and ask some of the world's most famous leaders, philosophers, and thinkers about what they think the key to a good life is!" Lara was grinning from ear to ear.

"I like that! Can we ask them other questions?" Tian asked, becoming excited, too.

"Sure, that's the point! They might help us find answers to what we're looking for."

"Cool! Like a treasure hunt, except through time and space! But wait... how are we going to get around? Planes? Trains? Buses?"

"All we need is the most *powerful* system of transportation: our *imaginations!*"

"We would need an ultra-light spaceship, but with special powers!" Tian said, excited about this unique trip. "We need to have that tree house we've been talking about for so long, Lara! The Indian tent can't be transformed into a spaceship!"

"If you look way down on that side of your grandpa's fence, there's a huge pine tree, which I heard has an old tree house at the very top—much larger than our old Indian tent! I bet that with your grandpa's tools, and our imagination, we can *totally* turn it into a spaceship!"

Not wanting to wait another minute, Tian yelled, "Yeah! Let's run over and check it out!"

Spiritual Passports

....

Lara and Tian arrived at the base of the huge pine tree, looked up to the top, and back to each other. They both smiled. In no time, they started to bring the things they cherished to the new tree house they had wanted for so long. Lara brought her seashells, flowers, and books. Tian brought his grandpa's tools to turn this tree house into the best spaceship ever. Nekty was also there, ready to start the adventure.

In no time, the old tree house was now the "spaceship" that would let them live their most memorable adventure.

"Can we use miles or coupons? I don't think my dad will give me any money for this trip," Tian said as he started using his grandpa's tools to make the tree house look like a real spaceship.

"We don't need luggage or tickets for our trip, silly!" Lara laughed. "We just need the unlimited power of our imagination and our *spiritual passports!*"

"I know that," Tian added, rolling his eyes. "I was just joking with you. But what are our spiritual passports? And how do we get them?"

"We will make them out of this recycled scrap paper!" She held up some old paper she'd brought with her.

"Tell me what they're for!"

"Every time we visit a place or ask a question, we'll get a stamp. The more stamps we get, the closer to our answers we'll be!" Lara happily explained.

"Great! Let's do it right now then!"

"Slow down, Tian, you're always rushing!" She smiled at him. "First, in order to prepare for our trip, we need to prepare *ourselves.* We'll meditate."

"Medi-what?" He yelled, making a face.

"*Meditate,* Tian. Me-di-tate." She sat and looked at him until he did the same. "Meditation is like going to sleep, but you stay awake. We breathe and keep ourselves quiet, so our minds can be at peace."

"Now, slow down," Tian said. He rolled his eyes. "I have *no* idea what you're talking about. Going to sleep, but *not* sleeping?"

Lara laughed a little. "Just *listen,* Tian. Let's close our eyes. We can even repeat a word or phrase to help us stop thinking of other things if that helps."

"Out loud?" Tian asked with his eyebrows raised.

"Quietly, to ourselves. Let's repeat, *I am calm, I am at peace,* while we slowly breathe in and out."

"I'll try...*I am calm, I am at peace. I am calm, I am at peace.*"

Lara and Tian both giggled. They meditated more and giggled more. After a while, they found themselves more than eight hundred years in the past.

Clara & Sebastian Naum

The Imaginary Journey

Ancient Rome
Marcus Aurelius—150 AD

"Hey, Lara, who's that old dude?" Tian pointed.

"That's Marcus Aurelius."

Without waiting, Tian asked, "Mister Marcus Aurelius, I want to know how to be happy all the time. What should I do?"

Marcus Aurelius responded, **"The happiness of your life depends upon the quality of your thoughts."**[1]

"Nice!" Tian exclaimed with excitement. "I like this guy." He turned to Lara. "Can we stay here in Italy and have some fun? We could eat some pizza and have some gelato! Happiness is, after all, the kind of thoughts we have, and we'd be super happy thinking about the pizza and gelato we were eating."

"Come on, Tian! The trip *just* started. We need to keep traveling and get some more good ideas. But before we leave Ancient Rome, we need to get our spiritual passports stamped!"

With their passports stamped, Tian and Lara hopped back into their spaceship and took off at light speed toward their next destination: Greece.

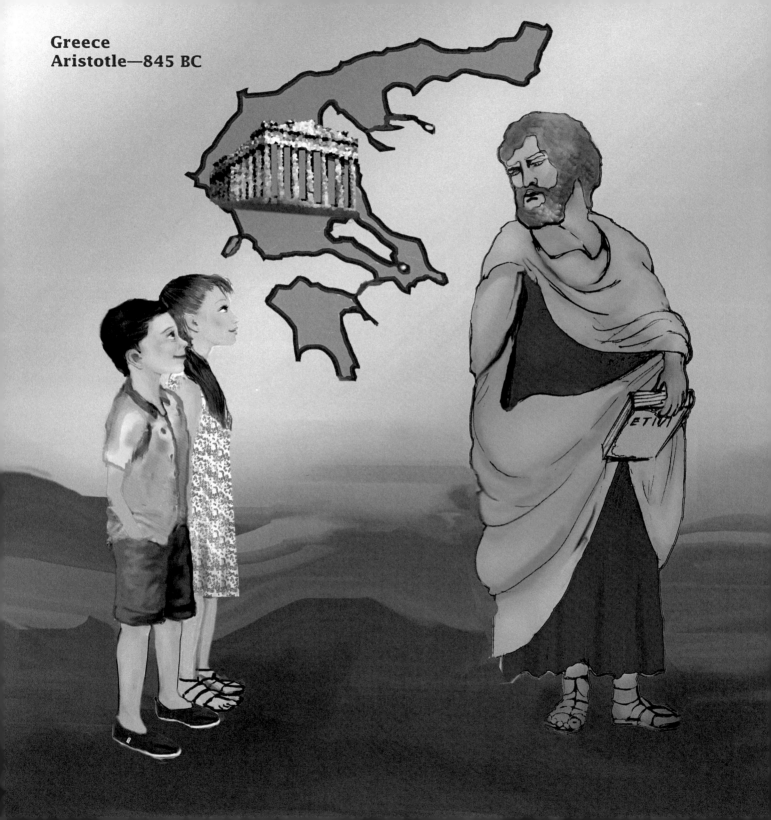

Greece
Aristotle—845 BC

"Who is that?" Tian asked.

"Aristotle, a *great* philosopher," Lara whispered.

"Excuse me, Mister Aristotle, may I ask you a question about life?" Tian asked, staring up at the man.

"Certainly," Aristotle replied.

"I want to be wise. What should I do?" Tian asked.

To this, Aristotle said, "**Knowing yourself is the beginning of all wisdom.**"[2]

"Wow, this dude seems to know everything! Let's get his opinion on happiness," Tian said to Lara.

"Do you doubt what Marcus Aurelius said, Tian?" Lara asked.

"No, I just wonder what this guy would say."

"Why not?" Lara smiled. "Mr. Aristotle, I have another question for you."

"Ask me, young girl," Aristotle answered.

"Where can I find happiness?"

"Happiness depends upon ourselves,"[3] he stated with a nod.

"What does that mean, Lara?" Tian asked with his face scrunched up.

"That we can *choose* to be happy," Lara said with a smile.

"Why, Lara? I don't get it."

"It means that we can *decide* to be happy!"

"Is it up to us?" Tian asked, still not very convinced.

"Yeap," Lara affirmed.

"Thank you very much, Mr. Aristotle!" they both said. "Goodbye!"

"Xaire!" Aristotle said, using the Ancient Greek word for goodbye.

"Oh! We have two stamps already. Now what, Lara?" Tian asked once they were back into their spaceship.

"Let's go to India!" Lara said as she bounced up and down from her seated position on the floor...

Tian nodded, and off they went to meet Buddha.

India
Buddha—500 BC

NEPAL
Lumbini

"Hush, Tian. Please. Buddha is talking." Lara held her finger to her lips.

"In the sky, there is no distinction of east and west. People create distinctions out of their own minds and then believe them to be true. It is better to travel well than to arrive."[4]

"How beautiful," Lara murmured softly.

"I don't get it. What's he saying? It doesn't matter how we arrive?" Tian frowned.

"No, it means that the most important thing is what we learn and experience during the journey, not the destination."

"Wow! I'm beginning to like this, Lara. It's getting more and more interesting. Let's get the stamp and go."

"Why don't we stay in India and travel in time?" Lara asked, without waiting for Tian's answer.

Lara and Tian got their spiritual passports stamped, and then traveled forward from 500 BC to 1963 AD in the blink of an eye!

India
Mahatma Gandhi—1963 AD

"Oh my goodness, look who's there!" Lara's eyes were open as wide as they could go.

"*Another* old dude. I think he needs a jacket, and maybe a cap to keep his head warm." Tian shook his head at the bald man in front of them who had the nicest smile.

"Tian...that's *Mahatma Gandhi!*" Since Tian looked puzzled, Lara went right up to the man and said, "Mr. Gandhi! Mr. Gandhi! How can we, as people, live better lives?"

"Hi there, guys," he greeted them. "Well, in my opinion, in order to live a better life, the most important thing is that **you must be the change you wish to see in the world.**"[5]

"Oh! I've never heard that before, but I think I get it...if I want to live in a better world, I have to *be* a better person!" Before Mr. Gandhi had a chance to continue, Lara asked, "Mr. Gandhi! Before you go...where can I find happiness?"

"Happiness is when what you think, what you say, and what you do are in harmony."[6]

"Thanks!" they said simultaneously. "Goodbye, Mr. Gandhi!"

"Namaste," Gandhi said, which was the Hindu way of saying goodbye.

"All right, Tian, since we are in India, let's go to Calcutta. I want to see Mother Theresa. My mom always talks about her!"

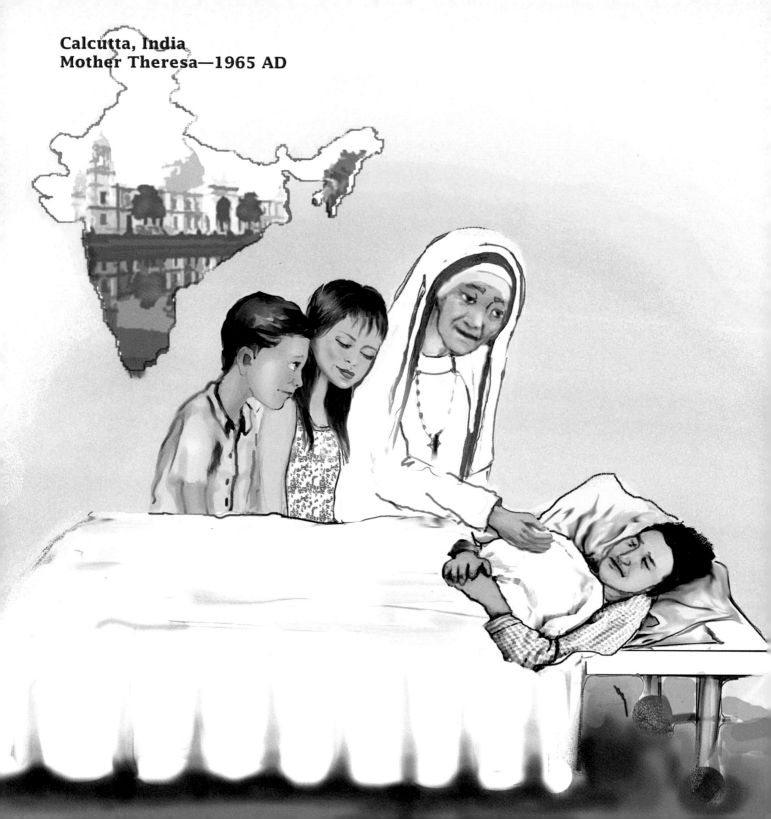

Calcutta, India
Mother Theresa—1965 AD

"Look, Lara, she's helping sick people." Tian pointed at the woman wearing a white and blue outfit and talking with people who were injured and sick.

"Tian, she is always helping"

"Is she a doctor?" he asked.

"No, she's a nun. For sure, one day she'll be a saint."

"Awesome! Let's ask her for some advice on life." He walked over. "Hi, Mother Theresa. We're from a faraway place and time and would love to hear your advice on life."

Looking at them with the kindest eyes, she said, "I love children and the best advice I can give you is, **people are often unreasonable, illogical, and self-centered. Forgive them anyway. If you are kind, people may accuse you of ulterior motives. Be kind anyway. If you are honest, people may cheat you. Be honest anyway. If you find happiness, people may be jealous. Be happy anyway. The good you do today may be forgotten tomorrow. Do good anyway. Give the world the best you have and it may never be enough. Give your best anyway. For you see, in the end it is between you and God. It was never between you and them anyway.**"[7]

"We want to tell everyone we know back home what you just said, Mother Theresa," Lara said in a trembling voice.

"We love you, Mother Theresa," Tian said, equally moved.

"Even though we already got our stamps," Tian said, "I still want to spend more time with Mother Theresa...I like the things she says."

"I know," Lara answered, nodding her head.

Still not ready to leave, Tian asked Lara, "Hey Lara, do you know who was the source of her inspiration?"

"The *master* of love, Tian! Jesus!"

"Oh, wow! But I bet visiting him would be impossible, right?" Tian asked, already a little discouraged.

"*Nothing* is impossible on this journey!" She smiled.

"Lara, I said it would be impossible because *he is* the *son* of *God!*" Tian exclaimed.

"Christians believe he's the son of God, but not the whole world. Nevertheless, everyone knows he was a man who lived in this world about two thousand years ago. He taught about love, humility, and mercy, regardless of anyone's religion. Imagine how important he was that we use the calendar years as before and after Christ!" **She smiled thinking about all that Jesus had taught.**

"Let's go back in time to the place he lived. I want to visit him now!" **Tian yelled.**

Jerusalem
Jesus—30 AD

All of a sudden, they were standing in front of the Wailing Wall. They looked to the left where a lot of children were seated listening to a man — Jesus was the one talking to those children. They were in awe and could barely speak to him.

Jesus turned to them and softly said, "Hi kids. It looks like you've traveled from faraway. What brought you here?"

They were both staring into his soft eyes. After a few seconds, Lara gasped and was finally able to articulate her thoughts. "Hi, Jesus. Yes, we're here because we want to know what *you* think is one of the most important things in life." Lara took a deep breath. "If there was just one message that we could take back home with us from you, what would it be?"

Jesus smiled and said, "**Love your neighbor as you love yourself**."[8]

Tian asked, "*Just* our neighbors, Jesus?"

Jesus, still smiling at them, said, "Everyone on earth is your neighbor, young man — the man living next door, the little girl begging on the street, the kid you don't like at school. *Everyone.* Become the children of peace." As soon as he said that, he left.

Lara and Tian waved and said, "Thanks, Jesus! We will!"

They were both silent for a bit, trying to keep the words they just heard inside their hearts and minds.

Lara and Tian were getting so many stamps and were learning so much, that Tian thought that after this past visit to Jerusalem, nothing else was left to see, and it was time to finish the journey.

"After all these trips, I feel that I have my answer. Let's go back home," Tian said.

"Not yet, Tian. I still have more questions. I also love to travel and meet new friends!"

Tian sighed. "Do you *ever* get tired?"

"Not during a great journey. I still want to meet more inspiring people around the world!" Lara laughed.

"OK, but let's at least get something to eat! I'm starving! Let's go to Iran and have some kabobs!" He licked his lips.

"No time for food, Tian!" **She laughed again and shook her head at how silly he was.**

"OK, but my passport is almost full."

"Don't even try that. A spiritual passport is *never* full and you can use it your *whole life!*"

"OK, OK. Let's travel to Iran now…and get those kabobs!"

Iran
Rumi—1,250AD

As soon as Lara saw the poet Rumi, she asked, "Where may I find love?"

"Your task is not to seek for love, but merely to seek and find all the barriers within yourself that you have built against it."[9]

"I don't get it, Lara." Tian frowned again.

"That means that we are *made* of love. We don't have to look outside of us, because love is already *inside* of us!" She smiled, despite Tian's obvious confusion. "I want to see another poet. I *really* like poetry."

"OK, but I'm *getting* more confused now." Tian shook his head.

"No worries. At the end of our trip, we'll find the answers we're looking for."

"Let's travel to Lebanon!" **Lara suggested.**

"Why Lebanon, Lara?"

"Because that's where the famous poet Khalil Gibran lived."

Lebanon
Khalil Gibran—1900 AD

"Mr. Gibran, please tell us about life," Lara said.

"Your living is determined not so much by what life brings to you as by the attitude you bring to life; not so much by what happens to you as by the way your mind looks at what happens."[10]

"Lara, this guy is *very* difficult to understand," Tian whispered.

"It means that not *everything* that we think is *bad* is *actually* negative unless we think of it that way."

"Lara, you're even more complicated than him!" Tian laughed.

She laughed and shook her head. "Just wait, and when you're upset about something, I'll explain it to you then, my friend!"

"Wait... I think I get it! It means that if we have a positive attitude *even* when bad things happen, we can live a happier life!" Tian exclaimed.

"Now what, Lara? I heard my father citing a Confucius guy from China ... and since I'm confused, let's travel to China and ask him something!" Tian said laughing.

Lara nodded her head and smiled back at him, thinking about how much she enjoyed the humorous things that came out of Tian's mouth at times.

This time they were taken directly to the heart of China 500 BC.

China
Confucius—500 BC

"Mr. Confucius, could you please tell us how we can find the ideal job?" Lara asked.

"Choose a job you love, and you will never have to work a day in your life."[11]

"Very clever. I like that idea, Lara. We just have to love what we do."

"Yes, this is getting better and better!" Lara smiled.

"Let's go back to modern times, Tian. Let's go to Africa and look for Nelson Mandela."

"Oh, I know that guy. He is in the movie *Invictus,* right?"

"*Finally* you know one of them! Yes, that movie is about him!"

In the blink of an eye, they found themselves in South Africa where Nelson Mandela was giving a speech.

South Africa
Nelson Mandela—2000 AD

"No one is born hating another person because of the color of his skin, or his background, or his religion. People must learn to hate, and if they can learn to hate, they can be taught to love, for love comes more naturally to the human heart than its opposite."[12]

"Mr. Mandela, please, I have a question for you. How do I find my mission in life?" Tian asked.

"There is no passion to be found playing small in settling for a life that is less than the one you are capable of living."[13]

Again, Tian frowned and scratched his head "I'm not sure…I find what Mr. Mandela says complicated."

"It may seem complicated, but it's not! We are *all* equal. We all have the right to do and create great things in this world. I feel like I'm starting to grasp it more and more clearly."

"Grasp what, Lara?"

"The answer!"

"OK, give it to me, please!" Tian begged.

"Not yet. We can still find some inspiration in our spiritual journey. Let's get our stamps and go!"

"Since we're already in Africa, we should go to Egypt. The answer may be in the Rosetta Stone."

Egypt
Rosetta Stone—196 BC

"I thought that the Rosetta Stone was a language learning software" Tian commented.

Lara laughed and smiled. "It is, but I'm talking about something much older than that."

"What *is* the Rosetta Stone, then?"

"The Rosetta Stone was an actual stone that was carved in 196 BC. It was written in three different scripts so that the priests, the government, the officials, and the rulers of Egypt at the time could read what it said and understand the hieroglyphics the Egyptians used! Isn't that amazing?"

"Yeah, I love learning about pyramids and Pharaohs. It's like an Indiana Jones movie!"

"Tian, this is *not* a movie. The Rosetta Stone is *real!*"

"Can we see it?"

"Yes, let's go now before going home!"

Tian was enjoying this adventure so much, that he didn't want to stop now. They traveled in time one more time and found themselves in front of the Rosetta Stone. They marveled at it, but after looking around, they decided that the answer was not there.

"What's next?" Tian seemed disappointed—his shoulders drooped. "We came here for nothing!"

"Sometimes we won't find everything we're looking for, but we learn along the journey anyway," Lara patiently explained.

"Is it play time yet?" Tian asked.

"Not yet. On our way back home, I'd like to say hello to Dr. Martin Luther King Jr. He was a great civil rights leader."

"Is he the one who said that every person is the same?"

"The very same."

On their way back to California, Lara and Tian made a quick stop in Atlanta, Georgia where Dr. Martin Luther King Jr. was giving a speech in front of thousands of people.

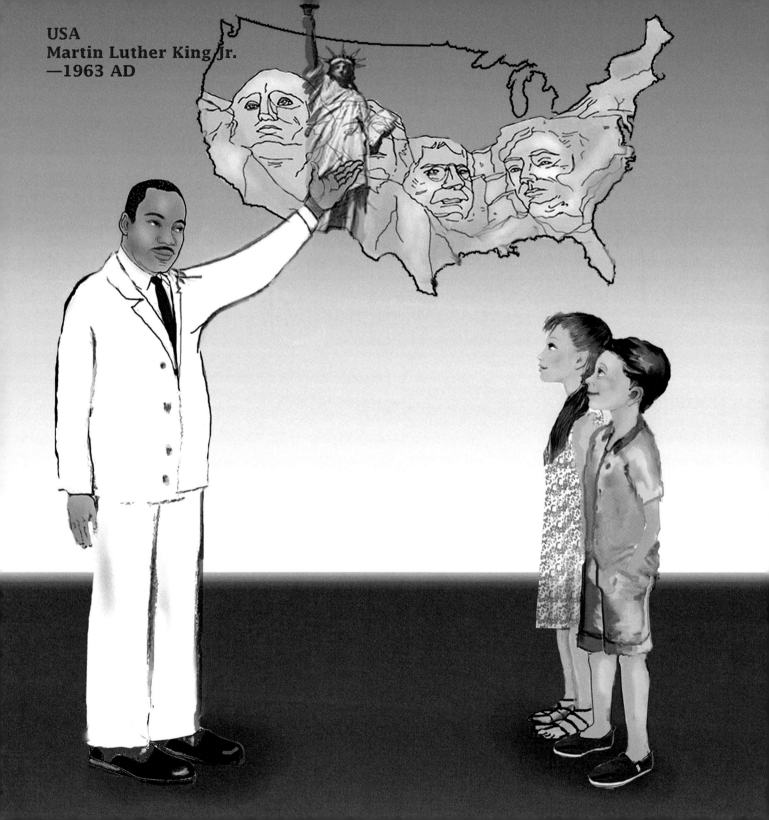

USA
Martin Luther King, Jr.
—1963 AD

"Darkness cannot drive out darkness; only light can do that. Hate cannot drive out hate; only love can do that."[14]

"His message is about being kind to each other, Tian."

"Yes, I really get it. It doesn't make any sense to hate people. It's better to love them. Let's get our stamps. We have a *lot* now."

They were fulfilled with everything they had listened to and the inspiration they had gotten. They were ready for their spaceship to once again become a simple tree house.

Lara opened her big eyes and said, "Tian , let's take one more *quick* stop to visit Helen Keller, and then I promise we will go back home. Please!"

Tian couldn't say no to his best friend.

USA
Helen Keller—1957 AD

Tian was a little anxious. He murmured, "How are we gonna ask her anything? She's deaf *and* blind."

"She knows how to communicate. She can read our lips with her hands! Isn't that awesome? She's an incredible and inspirational woman!"

Tian said, "Let's ask her how she can enjoy living without being able to hear or see."

Helen Keller smiled and softly said, **"The best and most beautiful things in the world cannot be seen or even touched. They must be felt with the heart."**[15]

They both smiled. "Thank you, Ms. Keller!" They both sighed and happily had their passports stamped for the last time.

Tian and Lara closed their eyes one more time, and using the power of their imaginations, they found themselves back home in California in their tree house.

They opened their eyes, sighed, and smiled again. "Mission accomplished," they both said. They looked outside the tree house and saw Nekty waiting for them patiently. They couldn't figure out how it happened, but Nekty was waiting for them with a seal hanging around her wrinkled neck, ready to stamp their spiritual passports as well.

The Answer

....

Lara and Tian were both happy and amazed about all the places they had visited, the people they had met, and all of the stamps they had collected. They began to realize that each of the stamps actually held the keys to living a better life. Their eyes sparkled like stars.

"Lara, did you notice that they all somehow talked about love and kindness?"

"Yes! And most importantly, the journey doesn't end here. We can use our spiritual passports to keep learning and traveling for the *rest* of our lives!" Lara sighed with a smile.

"So, wait...after all that, did we *even* find the answer?" Tian's shoulders dropped.

"Everything we have learned has helped us grow and led us to the place where the answer is."

"Where? Tell me, *where is the answer?*" Tian asked eagerly.

Lara smiled softly. "Inside of us."

"Inside of us?" Tian echoed

"Yes, we don't need to look outside. We learn, we get inspired, and we go inside of ourselves! **The answer is in our hearts!**"

THE END

...at least for now ...

Leaders, Philosophers, and Thinkers

....

Marcus Aurelius (121–180 A.D.)
Rome, Italy
Roman Emperor.

He was the last of the "Five Good Emperors." Known for his philosophical interests, he was one of the most respected emperors in Roman history. He was born into a wealthy and politically prominent family. Growing up, Marcus Aurelius was a dedicated student, learning both Latin and Greek, but his greatest intellectual interest was Stoicism, a philosophy that emphasized fate, reason, and self-restraint. Discourses, written by a former slave and Stoic philosopher, Epictetus, had a great deal of influence over Marcus Aurelius.

Aristotle (384–322 B.C.)
Athens, Greece
Greek philosopher and polymath, a student of Plato,
and teacher of Alexander the Great.

Aristotle founded the Lyceum, an educational institution, and was one of the most important founding figures in Western philosophy. Aristotle not only studied almost every subject possible at the time, but made significant contributions to most of them. In physical science, Aristotle studied anatomy, astronomy, embryology, geography, geology, meteorology, physics, and zoology. In philosophy, he wrote about aesthetics, ethics, government, metaphysics, politics, economics, psychology, rhetoric, and theology. He also studied education, foreign customs, literature, and poetry. His combined works constitute a virtual encyclopedia of Greek knowledge. It has been suggested that Aristotle was probably the last person to know everything there was to be known in his own time.

Buddha (563–483 B.C.)
Modern Day Nepal
Buddha Gautama, or Siddhartha Gautama Buddha,
a spiritual teacher from the Indian subcontinent,
on whose teachings Buddhism was founded.

He is the primary figure in Buddhism. Accounts of his life, discourses, and monastic rules are believed by Buddhists to have been summarized after his death and memorized by his followers. Various collections of teachings attributed to him were passed down by oral tradition and first committed to writing about four hundred years after his death.

Mahatma Gandhi (1869–1948)
India
Anti-war activist, prominent figure of the Indian independence movement, pacifist.

When asked to give a message to the people, he said, "**My life is my message.**"[16] Preeminent leader of Indian nationalism in British-ruled India, he employed the techniques on non-violent civil disobedience that he developed and led India to independence. He inspired movements for non-violence, civil-rights, and freedom around the world.

Mother Theresa of Calcutta (1910–1997)
Albania
Catholic nun and missionary.

She was born in Albania and lived in India. She devoted herself to caring for the sick and poor. She founded the congregation called the Missionaries of Charity. Her order established a hospice, centers for the blind, aged, and disabled, and a leper colony. In 1979, she received the Nobel Peace Prize for her humanitarian work. Pope John Paul II beatified her in 2003.

Jesus (circa 5 B.C.- circa 29 A.D.)
Jerusalem
The central figure of Christianity, whom the teachings of most Christian denominations hold to be the Son of God.

Jesus is also regarded as a major Prophet in Islam. Christians hold Jesus to be the awaited Messiah of the Old Testament and refer to him as Jesus Christ, or simply as Christ, a name that is also used secularly. Virtually all scholars of antiquity agree that Jesus existed. Most scholars also agree that Jesus was a Jewish teacher from Galilee in Roman Judea, was baptized by John the Baptist, and was crucified in Jerusalem on the orders of the Roman Prefect, Pontius Pilate.

Rumi (1207–1273)
Iran
Muslim poet, jurist, theologian, and Sufi mystic.

Rumi's importance is considered to transcend national and ethnic borders. His poems have been widely translated into many of the world's languages and transposed into various formats. In 2007, he was described as the "most popular poet in America."

Confucius (551–479 B.C.)
China
Chinese teacher, editor, politician, and philosopher of
the Spring and Autumn Period of Chinese history.

The philosophy of Confucius emphasized personal and governmental morality, correctness of social relationships, justice, and sincerity. He espoused the well-known principle: "**Do not do to others what you do not want done to yourself,**"[17] an early version of the Golden Rule.

Khalil Gibran (1883–1931)
Lebanon
Lebanese-American artist, poet, and writer.

Born in the town of Bsharri in Lebanon, as a young man he immigrated with his family to the United States where he studied art and began his literary career. In the Arab world, Gibran is regarded as a literary and political rebel. He is chiefly known in the English-speaking world for his 1923 book *The Prophet.* Gibran is the third best-selling poet of all time, behind Shakespeare and Lao-Tzu.

Nelson Mandela (born 1918)
South Africa
Civil Rights Activist, world leader, journalist.

He served as president of South Africa from 1994 to 1999, the first ever to be elected in a democratic election. Before being elected president, Mandela was a militant anti-apartheid activist. In 1962 he was arrested and convicted of sabotage and other charges, and sentenced to life imprisonment. Mandela went on to serve twenty-seven years in prison. Following his release from prison on February eleventh, 1990, Mandela led his party in the negotiations that led to the establishment of democracy in 1994. As president, he frequently gave priority to reconciliation, while introducing policies aimed at combating poverty and inequality in South Africa. Mandela has received more than two hundred and fifty awards over four decades, including the 1993 Nobel Peace Prize.

Martin Luther King, Jr. (1929–1968)
USA
American clergyman, activist, and prominent leader in the
African-American Civil Rights Movement.

He is best known for his role in the advancement of civil rights using nonviolent civil disobedience. In 1964, King received the Nobel Peace Prize for combating racial inequality through nonviolence. In the next few years leading up to his death, he expanded his focus to include poverty and the Vietnam War. He was posthumously awarded the Presidential Medal of Freedom in 1977.

Helen Keller (1880–1968)
USA
American author, lecturer, and political activist.

She campaigned for women's suffrage and labor rights. She was the first deaf and blind person to earn a Bachelor of Arts degree. She learned to "hear" people by reading their lips with her hands. A prolific author, Keller was well traveled and outspoken in her anti-war convictions. She spent most of her life giving speeches and lectures. She was inducted into the Alabama Women's hall of Fame in 1971.

Landmarks

....

Italy: Coliseum

Greece: Parthenon

India: Taj Mahal

India: Victoria Memorial

Jerusalem: Wailing Wall

Iran: Ruins of Persepolis

Lebanon: Beirut Raouche Pigeon Rocks

China: Great wall

South Africa: Maltese cross

Egypt: Rosetta Stone

USA: Statue of Liberty

USA: Mount Rushmore

References for Quotations

1 Marcus Aurelius

2 Aristotle

3 Aristotle

4 Buddha

5 Mahatma Gandhi

6 Mahatma Gandhi

7 Mother Teresa

8 Jesus

9 Rumi

10 Khalil Gibran

11 Confucius

12 Nelson Mandela

13 Nelson Mandela

14 Martin Luther King, Jr.

15 Helen Keller

16 Mahatma Gandhi

17 Confucius

Facts and information about the Philosophers, thinkers, and leaders mentioned in this book were gathered using information provided in Oxford Encyclopedia, Stanford Encyclopedia of Philosophy, and Encyclopedia Britannica.

About the Authors

··

Clara Leon Naum, M.A.

Clara, former CPA (Certified Public Accountant), holds degrees in Business, Sociology, and International Business and a Master's Degree in Spiritual Psychology from the University of Santa Monica. She is now a Spiritual Counselor, Certified Professional Life-Coach, and a soul-centered public speaker. Clara uses her own unique and innovative coaching style to help her clients live the life they love. She is committed to living and sharing the gifts of Spiritual Psychology. She dedicates time to volunteer in several causes. She is part of a team of graduate volunteers from the University of Santa Monica that has been bringing these principles and experiential practices to female inmates at one of the largest maximum-security women's prisons in the world—Valley State Prison for Women (VSPW). Clara also hosts an interactive radio show in Argentina called "How to live a better life" which helps thousands of listeners with their everyday issues and concerns. She is passionate about helping others achieve their dreams and traveling the world sharing her experiences and knowledge with others.

www.claranaum.com

www.facebook.com/sicologiaespiritual

Sebastian J. Naum

Sebastian is a successful Real Estate Broker in California. He is a former International Business liaison and holds a degree in Law and certifications in International Business, Marketing, and Public Relations from the University of California, Irvine.

He was a radio host in Orange County, CA for over eight years and an international correspondent for Radio Stations in South America.

While he is still working in the Real Estate field, in his free time he helps and supports his wife, Clara, so she can pursue her dream of publishing a series of books to inspire people to live better lives.

In addition to being a co-author of *Spiritual Passport,* he enthusiastically participated in the drawing and illustration process with artist Aida Shabani.

Through the voices of two children, Lara and Tian, the reader is taken on a round the world journey to the past in search of answers to some of our deepest concerns. In the straightforward manner that only children are capable of, Lara and Tian unveil the answers that we adults fail to see, simply because our minds and hearts have lost their ability to do so. This is a trip of discovery, an opportunity to appeal to the inner child inside each of us, and to remove our blindfolds. The truth is so simple that it seems magical. It will nourish your soul as it awakens your heart to the wisdom inside.

Made in the USA
San Bernardino, CA
09 November 2014